ANTHONY CROWLEY

THE BLACK DIARIES

ANTHONY CROWLEY

This publication is a work of fiction and any resemblance to persons, living or dead, or places, events or locales is purely coincidental. The characters are productions of the author's imagination and used fictitiously. This Book remains the copyrighted property of the author and may not be reproduced, scanned, or distributed for any commercial or non-commercial use without permission from the author. Quotes used in reviews are the exception. No alteration of content is allowed. If you enjoyed this book, then encourage your friends to purchase their own copy. Your support and respect or the author of this product is appreciated.

THE BLACK DIARIES

ISBN- 13-978-1497307759

ISBN-10: 1497307759

© copyrighted, 2014, Anthony Crowley & Crowley Creations

Edited by Simon Marshall-Jones (Spectral Press)

ANTHONY CROWLEY

The black diaries
Volume One

ANTHONY CROWLEY

ANTHONY CROWLEY

DEDICATION

I dedicate this work to the genius of what life represents and to the creative Artists of the past & present for shining an eternal light in us all

CONTENTS

Acknowledgments

The Conjuring Road   1

Resurrection   10

Ghost & the Raven   11

Constructing Death   12

Forgotten Asylum   13

The Sinister Train   15

Sunrise Bleeding   16

The Blackened Witch   17

The Nymph Garden   19

The Ripper   20

Shadow of the Wolf   22

Sleeping Village   24

An Interview with Anthony Crowley   29

Bibliography   32

About the Author   37

ACKNOWLEDGMENTS

I would like to thank, Paul & Andy & the team at Dead Good Publishing and also thank you to Steve Emmett, Julie Kavan & the Massacre Team, Catherine Cavendish, Horror Writers Association, UK HorrorScene.com, Oscar and Promotehorror, Dana Wright, Armada West, Richard Gladman, Jonathan Maberry, Jack Ketchum, Zachary & The Mouths of Madness, Ray Duchene & Terri King of Death Throes Publishing and thank you to Barry Skelhorn at Eye Trauma Press, Charles Bennett, Lauren Carroll, and many thanks & much appreciation to my followers and fans the readers who support the wonderful world that is Horror. If I have missed anybody you know who you are.

AC, October, 2014

ANTHONY CROWLEY

The Conjuring Road

'THERE COMES A TIME IN YOUR LIFE AND YOU THINK TO YOURSELF, WHY ARE WE ON EARTH FOR? IS IT SOME KIND OF GIFT OR A PRELUDE OF FATE?

Sitting down on an empty chair looking at those four walls surrounding you with a climax of thoughts or emotional cognizance, presently my mind is relaxed spontaneously; my name is Michael Sparks, not sure how my name came about, it must have been my father's idea, John Sparks He was a tall man with the greasiest hair, which may have been due to his fascination with rock and rock music. The neighbours feared him due to his focused, bloodshot eyes, resembling a wild animal ready to kill its prey. My father's skin was rough and rugged like tough, worn out leather, similar to a man twice his age. When I reached ten years old he disappeared, but my mother told me he'd gone on a fishing trip to Wales. As the days went by I found out that he was serving a life sentence in prison for arson and murder, and that he'd been sectioned on death row later on. My mother Betty was a glamourous woman, getting a lot of attention from strange people, but she thought she was as popular as a royal figure. Where I am living at this moment is not like any other location I have been to before, somewhere that tourists have never heard of. It was similar to an Indian reservation, protected and secure from the outside world, a holiday resort, except this was no holiday, and I felt as if I was living deep in a community of bloodthirsty sharks. The town is called Oakwood, a place which had once been occupied by Haitian slaves. The local gossip was that these people had been illegally shipped to Oakwood, forced to do strenuous work and subjected to abusive attacks in order increase agriculture and profits. There were rumours of incest. But there was one thing which fascinated me about these people above all; they believed in a form of a spiritual awakening. To escape the pain and torment they endured by practising Voodoo ritual magic.

I have only heard a few stories about Voodoo and the suffering it can inflict on the chosen victim I found the subject was widely feared but I also found it to be completely fascinating how it could change lives. I believe this form of magic to be a form of escapism from the depression which currently envelops me.

I'd, heard that these Haitian settlers had vanished during a storm, which happened over one hundred years ago now. At least that's what my ancestors had told me, but now I know differently. As I previously stated Oakwood was a town of lost souls: many arrived but none ever returned to the outside world. I now realise that I was living in a socially diseased place, hanging on the edge of an abyss. Many of the residents possessed a certain glow like a halo of light which hovered around them during every waking hour. It was soothing to witness, but I knew this supernatural light was something of an anomaly. There was only one safe location in the town I could escape to: the Quaker Hall, a shabby looking shack with rotten timbered window frames glazed with broken and filth-filmed glass, and masses of mould growing on the damp walls. It had been built by French colonists many years ago, but now the place was used as the local church, as well as a chapel of rest for the newly-deceased.

The priest in charge, Mr Pickles, was the 'High Priest', but the local people called him 'Mr P'. He was so named because it was rumoured that he pickled human body parts in order to purify the

soul. He was a very intelligent man, full of wit and vitality. He also spoke numerous languages, and knew a great deal about a variety of religions and philosophies. The villagers looked up to him like he was a god; he made everyone feel safe and secure. But that was soon about to change. The population had grown to fear and resent him, because of the magic he had studied and had hidden from them. . Mr P approached me and told me in a panicked tone;
   'Be careful my son, the whole village shall be damned and cursed'

'What are you talking about?' I replied confusedly.

   'I have to tell you something, something about this place' he told me quickly, 'This town was once a burial site for the hundreds of slaves who lost the lives for their beliefs; the torment these people had suffered was indescribably devastating. The only freedom they thought which would give them peace and serenity was to practice the art of Voodoo, but they eventually conjured something powerful and dangerous. They left behind a curse; this neighbourhood is now rapidly declining.' I was completely enthralled by what Mr P had related to me, but I was hesitant as to whether to pursue this further or escape while I still could. However, the mystery had me in its grip and so I decided to I wanted to know more about it to get some answers.

Thursday 30th April, 1979

I had gone for my usual walk around Oakwood; it was sunny, with a slight whispering breeze coming down off the nearby mountains. The day was completely silent, with not even an echo from the local birdlife. Despite that, I felt refreshed and revitalised. I arrived home two hours later, where I found mother busy in the kitchen.

   'Have you eaten yet?' she asked as soon as she saw me.

   'No, not yet'.

I knew what was coming: a ham and cheese my absolute favourite. While I was eating she asked me a lot of questions, reminding me of a cop drama.

'What have you been doing today?' she asked.

'I took a walk around town and met Mr P'

There wasn't much education here, though we did have Saturday school, the most boring thing you could think of.

'Stay away from that man Michael' she said, disapproval practically dripping off her tongue, 'he is not the saviour or man you think he is. His secrecy could destroy us all, including mine and your father's reputation, do you hear me?'
   The shrill tone in her voice worried me. Just now I felt confused and bitterly frustrated- I never knew just where I stood sometimes. I would frequently ask myself if I really knew my father, or even my mother? They're hiding something from me- don't know what the big secret is but I'm determined to find out!

Three weeks passed by

   The time was approaching 8am; I immediately dashed out up from my bed to the sound of running water along with the fragrance of Sandalwood and lavender. Just then my mother called to me.

'Michael, we have to see your father today. I had mail arrive unexpectedly saying that he's due to be released isn't that fantastic!'

'You told me he was on a fishing expedition? ' I replied

'It's pointless lying to you, but your Father did a bad thing and he was being punished for it' she said.

'What did he do?' I asked, a little upset at the news. 'I can't go into details even though I'd like to. I'll leave to your father to tell you.' responded my Mother. Like a lost puppy, I got up to go to the bathroom, the scents of lavender and sandalwood becoming much stronger. A thick haze of incense enveloped me as I entered the room where, to my amazement, I saw that my mother was standing in the centre of the tub surrounded by burning candles of black, red and green. I'd learnt many years ago that this was a ritual for spiritual protection. I notice patchouli leaves floating on the bathwater, the intense aroma making my eyes tear. My mother chanted and appeared to be in a trance, as if she were witnessing some kind of magical vision. Her nudity embarrassed me, her skin as pale as the moon. To make my shock even worse was the fact I'd never seen a naked body before.

'What are you doing mother?' I said.

She suddenly sat down on the edge of the tub, looking like she was about to faint.

'It's to prevent certain things from happening or, possessing you. It also replenishes your soul and wellbeing, you should try it sometime…?' she told me.

'Maybe one day' I responded.

We got dressed and made ourselves ready to make the long journey through sizzling heat and rough terrain to visit Father. He was imprisoned in a high-security facility called Cobb County Correctional Institute, housed in a building which looked forbidding, haunted and grey. Two cast iron gates at the main entrance loomed over us, resembling the entrance to a medieval castle. The air felt so humid and suffocating, and it made me realise why my Father was being punished here: there must be some secret he knew which could cause harm. As we walked under those iron gates, I noticed candles and small fires burning around the entrances to the corridors leading to the cells. Wisps of white smoke stung our eyes and flickering flames irritated our vision. I felt a little overwhelmed, and wondered why these fires and candles were here, but then quickly remembered that my mother had invoked spiritual protection earlier today.

I started feeling very scared, trembling with cold sweats, I feared the day of judgement was upon us, and that we were to become nothing more than forgotten dust. I began to hear chants, which became louder as we walked further through the mists of rising smoke along the narrow corridor. At this point, claustrophobia closed in on me: mother and I recognised the man sitting in shadow in the corner of his cell. We could only see a pair of piercing crimson eyes, and his breathing in the light of the flickering flames. He sat directly on the cold, cracked concrete floor encircled by black and white candles. He looked fragile even in the fitful light. Incense smoke swirled about like a protective cocoon, and a pentagram had been drawn on the floor. Next to his left hand side was set a small wooden mahogany table with brass legs, resting on the centre of which were a set of cards placed in the middle of a square of red velvet, I asked my Mother

'What's that Mother? What's he doing?' I asked, a touch of nervousness in my voice.

'Don't look at him, he's a voodoo witchdoctor, and on his table are his protections and weapons against evil.' Whispered mother in a hurried tone.

I was curious to know more about these strange cards and what they represented. 'What are those cards for, mother?' I asked, 'They are used a way to communicate with the dead and very powerful spirits from other worlds' she said in a reply.

I became afraid and scared then. The witchdoctor, looked directly at me, his eyes rotating in their orbits, while his trembling lips hummed an otherworldly melody. Without warning he stopped, plunging us all into silence.

'You are chosen, you are chosen' he said in a hoarse whisper.

Mother instantly grabbed me tightly, holding me fast by the wrist and hurrying me along the eerily echoing corridor. I sneakily turned my head to look behind me; the witchdoctor appeared in the blink of an eye, standing directly behind mother. He placed an icy hand upon my head, laughing like a devil from the deepest circles of Hell. Confusion swamped my conscious, temporarily frustrating

me. My thoughts felt as if they were being sucked out of my head. His grip on me loosened as my mother kicked him in the shin; he fell heavily, like a heavy rock, to the damp corridor floor. Taking the opportunity, we ran for our lives as fast as we could run, down this ever-spiralling passage. We could hear crows cawing and screeching in agony and pain. It sounded like a ferocious storm was rapidly approaching, thunder echoing menacingly outside the prison.
'Quickly, Michael, RUN! RUN!' mother screamed. 'They've come for us, they're here now !' 'Who's come?' I screamed at her, 'Tell me who they are!'

Eventually we reached the end of the corridor, and as if out of nowhere three strong-looking doors appeared in front us. We didn't know where father was held captive, so I began to call out his name but received no reply. I continued shouting, and not long afterwards I heard a faint voice.

'That's your father!' my mother exclaimed.

I was standing next to her and we both started kicking the middle door. Just as the door began to splinter, a gust of wind blew down the hallway carrying with it the voices of the dead slaves. The atmosphere changed, cooling dramatically, and still those voices crept closer. The force of the wind broke down the remnants of the door. We found father in the cell behind, apparently comatose; he looked like a zombie. This was the first time I'd seen him for some time- his appearance shocked me, but I knew we couldn't get sentimental as we were on borrowed time. The room was cold and clinically white. Father was stretched out on a hospital bed, lying quite still.

Just then we heard footsteps approaching outside the room. It was Mr P, clutching what looked like syringe. I remained steadfast next to father's bed, while mother began to question Mr P about what was going on.

'It was too good to be true, wasn't it? You just couldn't leave us alone since we moved into Oakwood. What are you trying to resolve? It wasn't our fault your ancestors were brutally tortured-

we have nothing to do with that. Just leave us alone, I want my husband back!' she shouted angrily.

'You knew what I wanted, but you wouldn't accept my offer, would you? Your beloved ancestors brutally savaged my family for success and greed, but they are back with us at last!' replied the sinister High Priest.

The atmosphere within the room dissolved into a motionless tableaux. My father looked terrified and feverish, staring fixedly at the entrance door. I followed where he was looking, to see strobing fluorescent beams darting everywhere and accompanied by voices, dark voices cloaked in a thick miasma of fear. We knew at that split second we had to act fast. My mother and I grabbed father from the bed and dragged him bodily into the mobility chair standing near the back end of the wall behind the bed. Mr P was in a trance, lost in the world of vengeful dead.

We briefly felt a moment of elation as we fled down the shadowed hallway to the exit of this forsaken building. Father began convulsions, his worn skin beginning to glow from the ritual drug he'd been forced ingest. He was no longer the Father I remembered from my distant memories of him. I attempted to open the exit door, but even though I was using my entire strength the door wouldn't budge. I felt weak and exhausted, suddenly aware that my body was fading into transparency. Relief hit as the door finally swung slowly open, creaking noisily as it did so. My mother laughed then, her expression becoming distant, and all three of us losing physical definition. But as our nature changed so did everything around us. The clouds thickened ominously with crimson scars cutting deeply through them.

Heaven appeared to be falling, fracturing the earth below; trees were blown around like matchsticks by a banshee wind. The ground shuck and shuddered violently. But even with all the noise I heard the dead chanting their song of victory. Red mists and orb-like spheres seeped out of the cracks of the ruptured ground. Mournful cries filled our ears, smothering our thoughts. I couldn't hear either mother or father, I was in a different world, distracted by the cursed storm raging around me. I spun around to see my parents had vanished.

I called out, but my voice faded into nothing. I was scared and numb with terror. I called my parents'- names they were faint, buried in the distance. I was lost within another realm, a realm unlike no other; I felt an uncanny urge to walk. I kept doing so in a straight line, searching for my old life perhaps, with my parents near me. I continuously called out their names. It felt like I was getting closer, but as I got nearer I felt it drifting further away. I had no strength left in me, and all I could do was wait. Waiting for home, but where was home?

© ANTHONY CROWLEY & Crowley Creations, copyrighted, 2014

Resurrection

Incredibly alone...

A place to hide
Thoughts are taken on the darkest ride
Gaze upon an isolated reflection
the devil can breathe... Crucified resurrection
World is empty, untrusted and cold
New dawn is coming, a mystical road…

One will testament the world shall see
A shadowed journey, the reality
The reality is thickening

Blackened with dust and bone
Suffering in silence
Fragmented and alone
Captured fire dreams
Terror in isolation
Armies of darkness
Infernal resurrection

© ANTHONY CROWLEY & Crowley creations, copyrighted, 2014

Ghost & the raven

Mystified...
Bewildered...
The darkness of the night
Awaiting for the ghostly sound
Of screams at the moonlight

Moments pass by

Hallowed bells ring out
Amongst the dead
Sunken hearts of a burial ground

Swollen fires from a Witches' sky
Torturous trees...
Flickering at nigh'
Sacrificial time
Endless isolated sleep
The Black Raven listens...
Distracting a mourning weep

© ANTHONY CROWLEY & Crowley Creations, copyrighted 2014

Constructing Death

Legendary vision
Mind propelling doom
Scientific thought
Transcending gloom

Medically curious
Chemistry illusion
Grave robbed corpse
Rebirth transfusion

Midnight experiment
Obituary withdrawn
Laboratory creation
Corpse tissue torn

Awakened monstrosity
Humane emptiness
Tall crept shadow
Anger & loneliness

Scar stitched tear
Spiralling nightmare
Daylight fear
Pale skin stare

Underground clinic
Mirror reflected soul
Construction of death
Darkness abode

© ANTHONY CROWLEY & Crowley Creations, copyrighted 2014

Forgotten Asylum

Whispered surroundings
Desolated walls
Partial shadows paint Demons
Upon the glistening creaked floor
Drugged, cleansed human
Insanely afraid
Comforting of devils
Seclusion man made

Darkest hour
Forthcoming shock treatment
A numbered cause for another replacement
Suffocated white jacket
Molested on chemical skin
Hallucinogenic appointment
Frightened maze within

Inflicted with fear
Nervously broken
Bruised red tears
Nightmarish token

Cell confined
Mentality abused
Doomsday watchmen
Blood Transfused
Captive moment
Sedated and strapped
Edge of darkness
Ferociously trapped

Screams of anger
Another denied day
Cries of pain
Prolonged stay

Shivering inside
Humanity sleep
Madness ride
Judgemental creep

Asylum abode
Sudden death weep

© ANTHONY CROWLEY & Crowley Creations, copyrighted 2013,2014

The Sinister Train

Strapped into a journey
The darkest of pleasures and dreams
The wheels are in motion
A tormented twisted departing
On this passage of fire and terror
no retreat to an unknown heaven
Heading for the devils causeway
An escape, a nightmarish haven

The rail tracks ablaze
From the deepened hallowed earth
Locomotive of infinity
Along this visionary turf
The lucid sky crumbles with clouds of forbidden grey
No rest for the wicked
Sinners will prey
Conductor of insanity
Passenger aborted, Lucifer rising

Stairway of dreamscapes
Forever in my stare
Prophecy of the future
Amongst the sinister lair
Destination of blasphemy
Reaching the Seventh gate

Stepping off the red masked train
A different world
Hell awaits

© ANTHONY CROWLEY & Crowley Creations, copyrighted 2014

Sunrise Bleeding

Mist filled hour
the fallen sky
distant sunrise
"I wonder why ? "

Blood trailed carpet
the killing floor
Lucifer's babies
hungered carnivore

Chariot of blackness
doorway of dreams
Midnight party
circled mass
Sunrise arrives
Bathory screams

© ANTHONY CROWLEY & Crowley Creations, copyrighted 2014

The Blackened Witch

I came upon this spiritual land for a chance to awaken new beginnings
My face and eyes are frosted pale ,since my innocent heart stopped forever beating
I am a shadow of my former self, enriched with words of divination and folklore
I believe in a higher destiny
A clearer path of thoughts and traditions of sorcery
The 'Book of Shadows' lay upon my illuminated and mystified altar
I draw down the wicked moon with wand in my hand
I am the forbidden priestess
Shall make my apocalyptic approach and I initiate thee I stand…

'Pentacle of Love, Shine so bright'
Pentacle of fire, give me eternal light'
I invoke the damned, and I will evoke with no curse on me or shame

Magus of fire, reaches out to me within
Phallus of evil and desire, shields around like a serpents blessed penetrated skin
I open up like a crimson flower from another wiccan world
My tempting chalice fills with goodness that I demand

The ritual has made me feel spiritually protected and attained
The general enters my circle and takes me in chrome weighted chains
I feel strong, yet weak, like a ghost in my veins
As I'm taken to my sentenced holy abode
A chilling chamber I leave ashamed

The fire rises higher, but a brightened doorway I can now clearly see
I sense strong burnt smoke and flaking sparkling ash
I have deep thoughts in myself, I am feared, but know my name
I am punished with the leathered whip of a lash
The general fears in denial to blame
I slowly drift now from this forsaken soil of Salem
I will live forever as one, my witchery of darkness shall appear again and again..

© ANTHONY CROWLEY & Crowley Creations, copyrighted 2013,2014

ANTHONY CROWLEY

The Nymph Garden

Fainted smile
an entombed kiss
enveloped with shivers
the luscious bliss

Etched heart
cold shallow womb
voyeuristic gathering
the garden womb

excitement with fairies
dancing around the pond
Victorian princesses
Old English underground

Sinful sinners
paradise of blue
shimmering & delightful
Gaelic fantasy of two..

© ANTHONY CROWLEY & Crowley Creations, copyrighted 2014

The Ripper

I drift slowly through the still of the night
Sounds of drunken laughter amidst the echoing of footsteps aloud
Another arousing temptation to end another life
Amongst the deadness of this dirty, filthy crowd.
Streets filled with sickness, decay and lower standards of humanity
'I have to butcher at least ten this evening to make it a fulfilling appetite'
The implements of death I have are a delight for my victim
The suffering arouses me, like a peaceful and cleansing momentous cure
I shall take her by the grasp of her throat, unknowing of what she'll endure..

I can feel her shivering at an alarming rate
Her soul drowns with bitter flooded tears
As her warm breathe begins to glow on this east end street…
I cut a deep incision into the skin under the breast
The venom of redness quickly flows down the slender of her milk white skin
I succumb to endless excitement, as I drag her across the mist-filled alley
I tear off her clothes revealing an innocent vision of dire lust
The crimson drops trickle slowly upon the frosted floor
Stitched together her dirty skinned labia

I gaze upon my victim with a twitch in my preying eyes,
The locals shall laugh no more, this gift I'll leave behind
This deceased surprise…..

I gather my blood stained tools while my stagecoach awaits..
They shall remember my darkened shadow
As I drift in the dead of the night
Through those hellish gates.

© ANTHONY CROWLEY & Crowley Creations, copyrighted 2013,2014

Shadow of the Wolf

It has emotionally felt like centuries
Since I was born innocently human
I now hide inside a carnivorous incarnation
My cries enrich for the dusk of the fallen night
Propelled my quickened thoughts for the blood thirst of arousing, tempting delights

I await the sudden frosted witching moon to climb the immortalised sky
Ambient surroundings as I scatter across the marshes and upon this holy land
The Hallowed mist shines upon my thickened dark-haired chest
Town voices I now hear before my sixth sense
Scattering through the crackling of hedgerows
Hard rain swamps under my tough blackened paws

I have crimson visions
As I hungrily enlarge with an evil looked stance
The flesh of the innocence with an ornamented stare so pure
Heaviness upon my galloping claws
I leap like a shielded canine with a suffocate of a gallant prance
Tearing upon the nerve twitched limbs
I tenderise the carcasses of humanity and slither the red raw emptiness of skin

Shattered bones array cross the muteness of the timid land
As blood stained dirt washes within my tiresome mouth
Sounds of the metallic horns, alerting my wild animal instincts
But never scare, I feel the growl within
I fade into the etched mist with my nocturnal predatory pose

ANTHONY CROWLEY

Mental shadow I left behind
Scavenging through the twilight of night
Visions of my crimson clot eyes
Trembled with fear and stiffness-like froze
Another feast upon me now
This time firstly I'll devour their pulsating toes…..

© ANTHONY CROWLEY & Crowley Creations, copyrighted 2013,2014

Sleeping Village

"I can still hear those crashing sounds of the approaching winds, sounding like a wailing banshee as I am taken along this dirt swamped passage to a new resting place in a man-made Gothic structure, a tower of solitude, a turmoil of forbidden dark depths amongst the awakening of a whirlwind of compelling visions of entrapment with the remembrance of who I am in this isolated new world"

I can still recall the terrible cries when the village Doctor came to my family home on that dreary winter's day of the year 1348. The village has now become a sleepy residence, piled with decay upon decay, peopled with the dead and the souls of the lost. Even the local tradespeople had suffered considerable loss, and they soon deserted this fallen community and travelled disguised as highway thieves to the next village. I came from a family of seafarers and merchants, my ancestors having worked extremely hard, trading fresh sea bass and the tastiest, most exquisite caviar along the Cornish fishing coastal town of Penzance. The days ahead were bleak and full of unknown fears; fears you dare not dwell upon, unless it affect your thoughts of desperate survival until the instant death took you in its cold black grip.

'My name is Sir Edward Fitzroy Fuller. My family came to England from Croatia, with a fortune large enough to continue their legacy in this great land of hope and glory. My parents were a different class of society, an aristocracy if I may say, many of the locals thinking they thought themselves much better than everyone else. My mother and father were known as Sir Edgar and Lady Luna Petrovik, Sir Edgar told me that as a young boy he would observe the moon for many long hours, having an interest in Astronomy. When he was introduced to my mother at a lavish dinner party for the wealthy, he was astonished that her name translated to 'moon' in English, and so they fell in love. My parents were extremely wealthy, funding the European Parliament to assist its growth and production'.

But greed became the better of this devious, rebellious government. My family were attacked and were threatened with alienation and were made to feel like strangers in a strange land during those dark days, which presently grew much worse. Once blue skies became filled with rising clouds of doom, presaging a day of judgement. The day broke with the rustling sound of chains heavily beating against the cracked floor, Edward sitting perched in the corner watching the blood-stained rat burying its teeth into the corpse of another victim of this ill-starred disease. Edward felt a sudden sadness while experiencing a reflective moment that this corpse could have been him.

The air within this small cell was at a minimum, only two holes in the ceiling allowing air to flow in. Edward knew that black crows would sweep down into the tower's to feast upon the dead husks of the villagers. Sunrise came early today at 03:00, instead of 05:45. Edward felt mounting desperation, and the need to free himself from this tower of infernal death. The air became more stifling, the suffocating stench of rotting flesh which wafted from the surrounding marsh pushing down on him. The thickening residue oozing from the bodies of the drifting and dying began to change colour as it turned the cold concrete floor into a quagmire of decay. The only entrance to the tower was via a creaky wooden drawbridge, constructed to keep out the woodland dwellers who had a history of cannibalism and bizarre bloodsoaked rituals. Edward had a moment's thought, recalling that when he was captured he couldn't remember seeing his parents. He knew he had to free himself from the iron clasped chains keeping him captive. Edward had a sudden rage, quickening his strength, knowing he had to flee from this tower full of decomposition. He had attempted several times to break the heavy iron chains but with no luck. The smell of blood was now becoming intensely cloying, and only a few yards from his weakened feet there lay the body of the fisherman, its ribcage open like a gutted fish waiting to be eaten. Edward had an idea; there was a small bone located on the lower rib which he could use to pick and unlock himself from the weighted chains holding him. Edward kneeled on the floor next to the rotting cadaver and tried to ease the bone away from the ribcage, but the bone refused to come away from the corpse. His worst fear instantly struck inside Edward's mind like the jaws of a vicious man-trap. He moved his wrists closer to the cracked rib, and managed to loosen one of the iron chains. Edward pulled quickly without hesitation and, the split second he freed himself, he heard a sound of footsteps echoing up the stairwell within the tower, as well as the out of place sound of a flute being played. It was one of the local woodland dwellers, people of a short height and disfigured facial features. Nobody had known about their existence until the day came when a local village fete was being held and the villagers had noticed that several children had disappeared under strange circumstances, which led to speculation of cannibalism. Edward quickly undressed from the blood-stained rags he was wearing and took the clothes from the dead body lying next to him, but the fabric was stuck to the stinking putrid flesh of the corpse. He was now fuming, panting with exhaustion, and overwhelmed by his desire to escape. He pulled and pulled until the skin came off the body like fruit peel. It was the only option he had to disguise himself from the forest-dwellers. The door began to open; the shaking and metallic shuffling of the keys signalling that someone was coming in. He smelled death and saw the look of hatred as the local dweller walked whilst banging his feet upon the floor. The saliva dripped from his mouth like slavering beast and those teeth were sharp as those of a wolf's. Luckily for Edward the woodland dweller hadn't recognised who he was, lost in a daydream as he was while feasting upon the four dead bodies in the cell. Edward ran fast as he possibly could down the tower's spiral steps. The breeze hit his pale face like a thunderous blow and, as soon as he reached the end of the stairwell, the raucous sound of black crows called a song of pain and suffering. Relief dawned upon Edward. He forced his way through the cast iron entrance door, and to his amazement he saw his parents standing still on the other side of the elevated drawbridge. Their frozen stares looked right through their beloved son, with neither a shred of sadness or remorse, but a time for his parents to be proud of their vicious method of gains and successes. Evil laughter erupted from them. Edward was horrified, questioning the reason why he'd come to this conclusion: he wanted to be loved, to be set free and be as a big success as his parents and ancestors.

'We are sorry, son we did this for us, knowing that by law you would have gained everything and we couldn't let that happen!' Edward's mother, Lady Luna, said greedily.

'This isn't happening, it can't be!' replied Edward.

'Don't you get it? We knew the meat market was shrinking, but our ancestors believed in us and so we had to be bigger than they'd been to make them very proud' Lady Luna continued...

The whole world around Edward collapsed. He felt the razor-sharp blade of truth in what he heard, the devastating expression on the child-like face of Sir Edward revealing he knew what meat was being used. The village was now quiet, with no one to be seen or heard; only the vision of slow, decaying death and the sickening song of the black crows and the town dwellers as they ate the remains of the bodies. There was no escape and no way out, just the simple presence of fear and death, while the sun slept.

© ANTHONY CROWLEY & Crowley Creations, copyrighted 2014

THE BLACK DIARIES

Interview 2013

An Interview with Anthony Crowley

After conducting this interview, I decided that a typical Q&A format would not do justice to this interview. Mr Crowley is not your run of the mill writer so why have a run of the mill interview right?

We spoke over Google hangouts and it was excellent to not only hear what he had to say, but to experience how he said it. He has a depth of personality that presents itself not in his work, but in his person. To hear him explain where he draws his motivation from is enlightening to say the least. He is a man who has taken the past and turned it into a beneficial future.

As a child, Mr Crowley was exposed to classic works and to this day quotes his favourites to be the great Peter Cushing and Christopher Lee. The traditional black and white horror films continue to represent the truest nature of the genre for him. His grandfather was also a poet and Mr Crowley is proud to say it impacted him on a level that will likely remain with him for the rest of his life.

When asked about where his inspiration comes from now, he explained to me that he perceives his mind as a very large house with many doors. Behind each door lurks a story waiting to be told and all he has to do is open the door. Sometimes a thought will come to him and it either floods his mind with the entire story (or poem) or he jots down the thought before sleeping. When he wakes again, the entire story is there, even if it happens at three am. There are times when he feels he has to pull himself back because he is strapped into a train and it's moving continuously, laying down tracks of stories and poems to be told.

There are times when he will start with a title only and it tells itself. The experience is surreal, just as his recent success has been surreal to him. He describes it as a break from the past in which he had been afraid to be himself (as most people are) because it would make people go away. When he realized he couldn't truly be happy until he was himself, he broke free of the past and pursued what makes him happy. "Wheels of Damnation" is his work about being afraid and the pain of disruption on his path to becoming his true self.

His past life varied from being a member of the British Forces to indulging in the occult. He has used all of his life experiences to shape who he has discovered himself to be. He applies to his work in using the emotional and psychological tactics of writhing. Fear and feeling can be presented to people; however, they have to draw it from the work. He feels a writer cannot simply tell a person how to be afraid, thus play on the emotion and psyche are imperative. "The Ripper" was described by Mr Crowley as being used to 'test the waters' when he submitted to a publisher in New York, U.S. It was rejected as being too graphic for the publishing house but he persevered, and it has been picked up by Massacre Magazine for publication.

His method has proven to work well for him. His recent poetry has developed a very strong following and inundated him with contacts from magazines, webzines, and podcasts. "The Fallen Angel" was broadcast on Dr Snake—Voodoo Witch Doctor and within the same day "The Devil's Foot Soldier" (inspired by 'The Orphan Killer movie and well received by the creators of the 'Slasher Icon' movies) was featured in Blood Born Magazine. He finds both experiences amazing. As I said, just reading the words won't convey the honesty of what I was able to experience by speaking with him, his sincerity over being thrilled and the surrealism of it all are very apparent by his demeanour. A look at his author Facebook page is only a drop in the bucket of his recent success. He also has a new novel due out by the end of the year and is continuing on his "bullet ride" of writing.

www.facebook.com/AnthonyCrowley.Author

Mr Crowley also has a lifelong passion in the music industry. He has developed a talent for writing song lyrics which he explains helped while attending Music College in Birmingham and led to him becoming a seasoned entertainer in more than one creative medium. I certainly didn't expect to hear, but was pleasantly surprised, that he is writing music for an artist here in Canada as well. So what truly scares a man who delves into the psyche of the mind to develop horror?

He tells me it's still the fear of the unknown that was instilled in him as a child when he watched, believe it or not, *The Elephant Man*. The fact it was real, but at the same time an unknown reality, he described it as "terrifying".

With all of that said, Mr Crowley is humbled by his success and is by far one of the most pleasant and inspirational people I personally have ever spoken with. I can't thank him enough for his time and openness with me.

-- Interview feature, December, 2013 special © Death Throes Publishing 2013, 2014

Interview conducted by Terri King of 'Death Throes

Originally sourced at www.deaththroes.net/anthony-crowley-interview.html

"Many thanks & much appreciation to Death Throes & Terri King" – AC

Anthony Crowley Bibliography

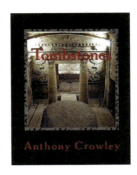

TOMBSTONES (*Anthology/ collection*)

ISBN-978-1495992315 ASIN: B00ITEXMC2

published: 5th March 2014

Tombstones is a collection of some of the finest dark verse and Horror themed literature, whilst exploring the various elements of dreams, Erotica, Psychology and complete fear... Including the popular dark verse 'The Fallen Angel' and the powerfully erotic vampire tale of 'Blood Hungry'.

Available from all good book stores
(8.5 x 11) CRYPT edition also available

The Light of Keeps Passage

ISBN-978-1497598898 ASIN: B00JL0P6AE

published: 9TH April 2014

The Light of Keeps Passage is a Supernatural tale about one boys escape for a better life and fulfilment, but something more mysterious awaits.
Frank Dracen, is a regular schoolboy who wants to escape his miserable life from his empty home and ignorant family. He begins to have visions with a mystical nature.
In a modern world full of total control, he has his dream come true, Frank Dracen eventually has a way out of all his problems.

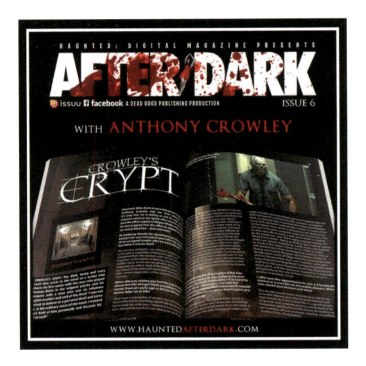

Check out CROWLEY'S CRYPT in Haunted after Dark

OUT NOW!

® Haunted after Dark magazine is published & owned by © Dead Good Publishing 2014

ANTHONY CROWLEY

THE BLACK DIARIES

ANTHONY CROWLEY

ABOUT THE AUTHOR

Anthony Crowley (born 1979, Birmingham in U.K). From a young age, Anthony began to take an interest in English literature and poetry from early childhood. Then throughout his teenage years he studied music and developed his song-writing skills, whilst still creating his visions. He also achieved a diploma in creative writing with a college located in Oxford, England. Anthony has also written short stories for student newsletters and horror monthlies. In the present day Anthony Crowley is a featured contributor to *'Haunted after Dark'* with his very own dark haven of 'Crowley's Crypt' and has written many works of literature & poetry for publications, such as, *Massacre Magazine, Sanitarium, HelloHorror*. The dark verse of *'The Fallen Angel'* featured in *Sanitarium Magazine* issue 14. The work itself was mentioned via a live radio podcast on the evening of Halloween 2013.

'The Devils Foot Soldier' was another dark verse which was inspired by the *Slasher Icon* movie of 2011 *The Orphan Killer* which was positively recognized by the movie's creators and the written piece is now featured at US-based *Blood Born Magazine*. He is highlighted in several more features and frequent media interviews and being ranked as "one of the best Modern Authors in recent years". Horror-Web described him with the following statement 'Anthony Crowley is one of the most prolific and talented authors of dark prose and poetry'.

During a recent interview on *Sinister Scribblings* Mr Crowley has been placed amongst the likes of Poe, Lovecraft and Clarke Ashton Smith. Forthcoming Novella *The Mirrored Room* was ranked in the semi-finals in the 'AuthorsdB' Book Awards of 2013, and ranked four times in the 'Top 100' list of popular authors, not forgetting that he was a trending author for many consecutive months and a featured author on numerous literature and horror-themed websites and more.

Presently, Anthony Crowley has published the best-selling horror anthology *Tombstones* and the introduction to a new dark series *The Black Diaries*.

Anthony Crowley dubbed "the Master of Realities" is always creating new and exciting projects within the genres of speculative literature and Horror, Occult and Historic references.. Anthony is currently resides in England

ANTHONY CROWLEY

THE BLACK DIARIES

ANTHONY CROWLEY

THE BLACK DIARIES

ANTHONY CROWLEY

Made in the USA
Lexington, KY
18 March 2015